"一只小老鼠，叽布叽布，在密林深处溜达。
一只狐狸看到他，馋得口水直滴答……"

请你跟着小老鼠，
走进这茂密的森林。
看看这只聪明机灵的小老鼠，
碰到了不怀好意的狐狸、猫头鹰、蛇，
还有那大怪物咕噜牛，
他是怎么样一一对付……

京权图字：01-2020-3528

Text Copyright © 1999 Julia Donaldson
Illustrations Copyright © 1999 Axel Scheffler
The original edition is in English and published by Macmillan Children's Books, London.
This edition is for sale in the People's Republic of China only, excluding Hong Kong SAR, Macao SAR and Taiwan Province, and may not be bought for export therefrom.
本产品只限中华人民共和国境内（不包括香港特别行政区、澳门特别行政区及台湾省）销售。不得出口。

图书在版编目（CIP）数据

咕噜牛 /（英）朱莉娅·唐纳森（Julia Donaldson）著；（德）阿克塞尔·舍夫勒（Axel Scheffler）绘；任溶溶译．－－北京：外语教学与研究出版社，2020.10（2024.12 重印）
（聪明豆绘本：中英双语版.《咕噜牛》作者经典绘本系列）
书名原文：The Gruffalo
ISBN 978-7-5213-1998-9

Ⅰ. ①咕… Ⅱ. ①朱… ②阿… ③任… Ⅲ. ①儿童故事－图画故事－英国－现代 Ⅳ. ①I561.85

中国版本图书馆 CIP 数据核字（2020）第 141351 号

出 版 人　王　芳
策划编辑　赵兴亚
责任编辑　汪珂欣
责任校对　刘毕燕
封面设计　卢瑞娜
出版发行　外语教学与研究出版社
社　　址　北京市西三环北路 19 号（100089）
网　　址　https://www.fltrp.com
印　　刷　天津市银博印刷集团有限公司
开　　本　889×1194　1/16
印　　张　2.5
版　　次　2020 年 10 月第 1 版 2024 年 12 月第 6 次印刷
书　　号　ISBN 978-7-5213-1998-9
定　　价　28.00 元

如有图书采购需求，图书内容或印刷装订等问题，侵权、盗版书籍等线索，请拨打以下电话或关注官方服务号：
客服电话：400 898 7008
官方服务号：微信搜索并关注公众号"外研社官方服务号"
外研社购书网址：https://fltrp.tmall.com

物料号：319980001

聪明豆绘本·中英双语版

《咕噜牛》作者经典绘本系列

THE GRUFFALO
咕噜牛

[英]朱莉娅·唐纳森 著　[德]阿克塞尔·舍夫勒 绘　任溶溶 译

外语教学与研究出版社
FOREIGN LANGUAGE TEACHING AND RESEARCH PRESS
北京 BEIJING

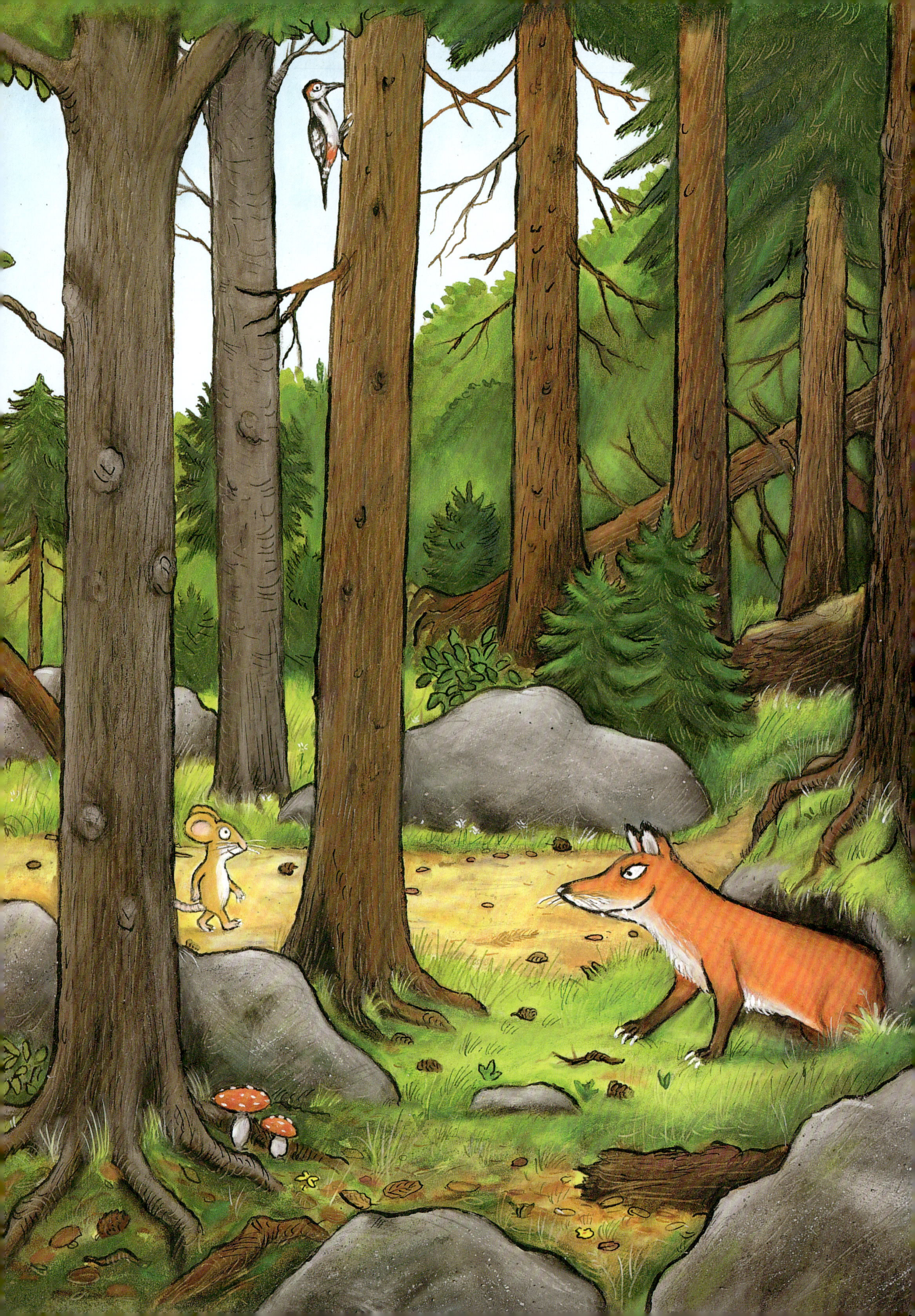

一只小老鼠，叽布叽布，在密林深处溜达。
一只狐狸看到他，馋得口水直滴答。
"亲爱的小老鼠，你要上哪儿啊？
进来吃顿饭吧，树底下就是我的家。"
"哦，狐狸，你太客气啦！可是很抱歉——
咕噜牛约我来吃饭，一会儿就见面。"

"咕噜牛？咕噜牛是谁啊？"狐狸问道。
"咕噜牛就是咕噜牛！怎么，你连这也不知道？"

"他有可怕的獠牙，

可怕的爪子，

可怕的嘴里长满了可怕的牙齿！"

"你们要在哪儿见面？"
"就在这块岩石旁边。
烤狐狸这个菜他最喜欢！"

"烤狐狸？对不起，小老鼠！我还有事要先走！"
狐狸说着，飞也似的就开溜。

"这只狐狸真是蠢！什么咕噜牛！
难道他不知道，咕噜牛根本就没有？"

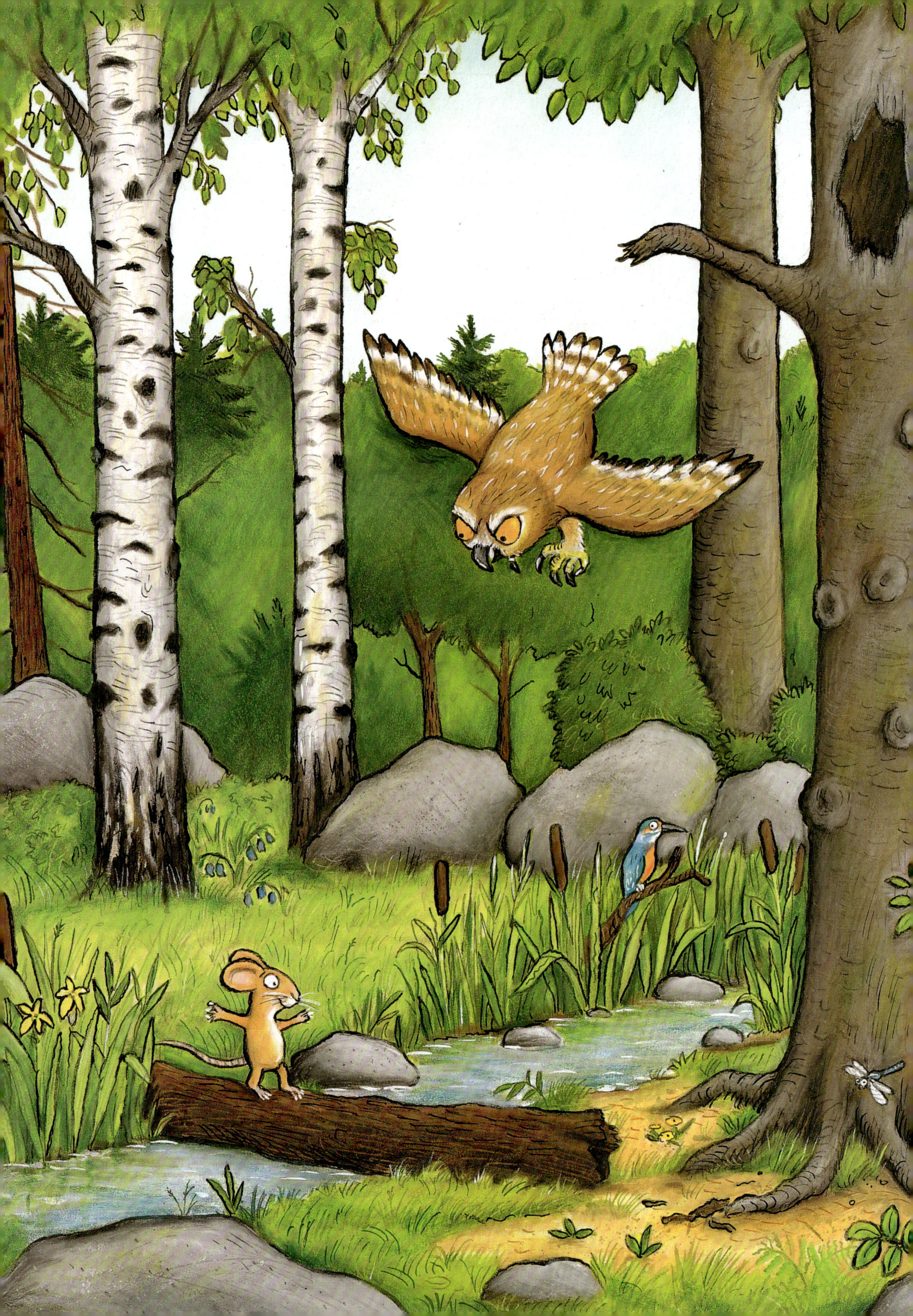

这只小老鼠，叽布叽布，继续在林中溜达。
一只猫头鹰看到他，馋得口水直滴答。
"亲爱的小老鼠，你要上哪儿啊？
上来喝杯茶吧，树洞那儿就是我的家。"
"哦，猫头鹰，你太好心啦！可是很抱歉——
咕噜牛约我来喝茶，一会儿就见面。"

"咕噜牛？咕噜牛是谁啊？"猫头鹰问道。
"咕噜牛就是咕噜牛！怎么，你连这也不知道？"

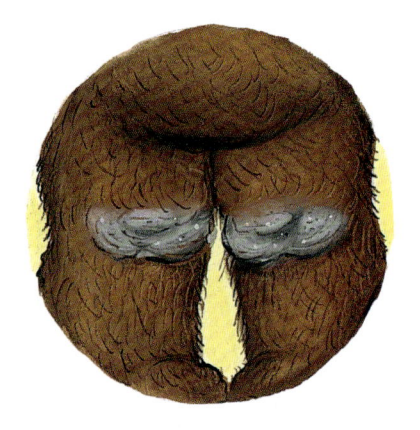

"他的膝盖特别鼓，

脚趾叉得特别大，

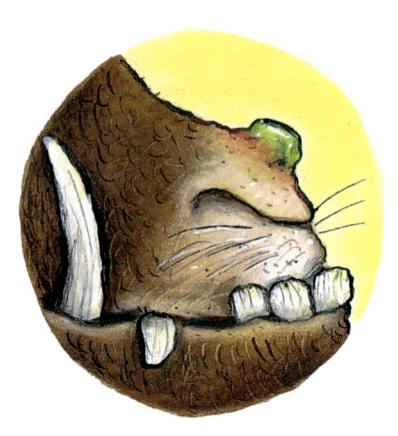

鼻头上的毒瘤特可怕！"

"你们要在哪儿见面？"
"就在这条小河边，
　油炸猫头鹰这个菜他最喜欢！"

"油炸猫头鹰?对不起,小老鼠!我还有事要先走!"
猫头鹰说着,拍拍翅膀就开溜。

"这只猫头鹰真是蠢!什么咕噜牛!
难道他不知道,咕噜牛根本就没有?"

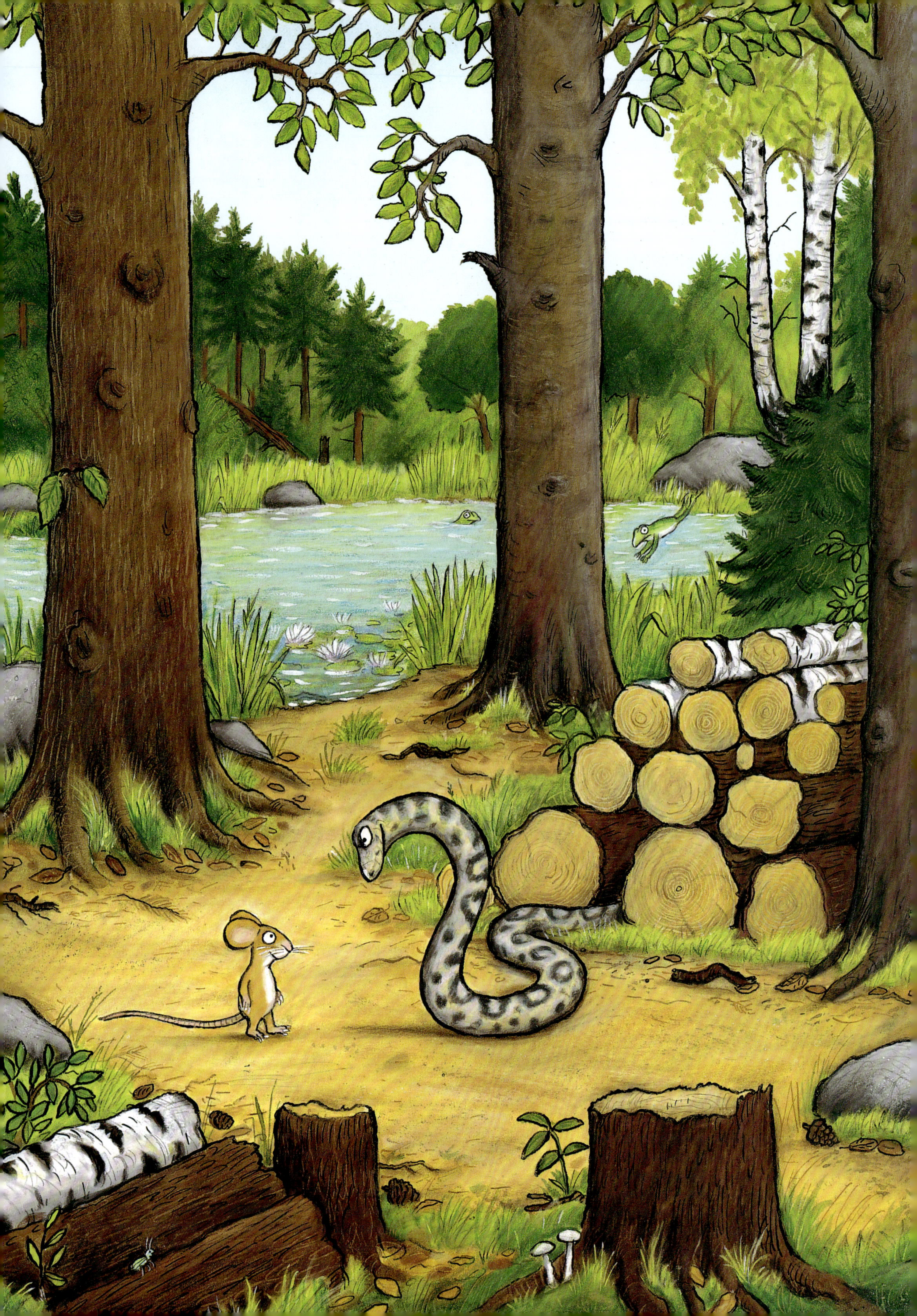

这只小老鼠,叽布叽布,继续在林中溜达。
一条蛇看到他,馋得口水直滴答。
"亲爱的小老鼠,你要上哪儿啊?
 进来喝杯酒吧,木头堆里就是我的家。"
"哦,蛇,你太热情啦!可是很抱歉——
 咕噜牛约我来喝酒,一会儿就见面。"

"咕噜牛?咕噜牛是谁啊?"蛇问道。
"咕噜牛就是咕噜牛!怎么,你连这也不知道?"

"他有黄澄澄的眼睛， 黑舌头，

紫色的倒刺长满在他背后。"

"你们要在哪儿见面？"
"就在这个湖旁边，
 炒蛇肉这个菜他最喜欢。"

"炒蛇肉?对不起,小老鼠!我还有事要先走!"
这蛇说着扭着身子就开溜。

"这条蛇真是蠢!什么咕噜牛!
难道他不知道,咕噜牛根本就……

"……哎哟!"

哪来这么个大怪物——
他有可怕的獠牙,可怕的爪子,
可怕的嘴里长满了可怕的牙齿!
他的膝盖特别鼓,脚趾叉得特别大,
鼻头上的毒瘤特可怕!
他有黄澄澄的眼睛、黑舌头,
紫色的倒刺长满在他背后。

"哦,不,不,不!救命啊!怎么真有……
怎么真有……**咕噜牛**?"

"我最爱吃小老鼠！"咕噜牛说道，
"弄个老鼠汉堡，味道肯定非常好！"

"味道好？你先别说我味道好！
有件事情，恐怕你还不知道。
在这林子里，大家怕我怕得不得了。
只要跟我走一圈，马上就让你看到，
他们个个见了我，吓得全都赶紧逃。"

"那我倒要开开眼!"咕噜牛哈哈大笑,
"你在前面走,我跟在你后面瞧。"

一小一大往前走,咕噜牛忽然停下,
"草丛里面嘶嘶响。你可知道那是啥?"

"一定是那条蛇在爬。"小老鼠说,"蛇啊蛇,你好!"
蛇抬起头,把咕噜牛瞧了瞧。
"哦,我的天啊!"他说,"我得赶紧把命逃!"
哧溜溜他就不见了。

"看见没有？"小老鼠说，"大家见我都逃跑！"
"这事还真是有点儿怪！"咕噜牛说道。

一小一大继续走，咕噜牛忽然又停下，
"树梢顶那儿咕咕响。你可知道那是啥？"

"一定是那只猫头鹰在叫。"小老鼠说,"猫头鹰,你好!"
猫头鹰低下头,把咕噜牛瞧了瞧。
"哦,我的妈呀!"他说,"我得赶紧把命逃!"
呼啦啦他也不见了。

"看见没有?"小老鼠说,"大家见我都逃跑!"
"你还真是不得了!"咕噜牛说道。

一小一大继续走,咕噜牛忽然又停下,
"前面路上啪啦响。你可知道那是啥?"

"一定是那只狐狸。"小老鼠说,"狐狸,你好!"
狐狸抬起头,把咕噜牛瞧了瞧。
"哦,救命啊!"他说,"我得赶紧把命逃!"
转眼间他也不见了。

"看见没有，咕噜牛。"小老鼠说道，
"他们个个见了我，全都吓得赶紧逃！
溜溜达达走半天，我的肚子早饿啦！
听说咕噜牛肉很不错，我倒真想尝尝它！"

"咕噜牛肉！"咕噜牛一声叫，
快得像风，他转身就逃！

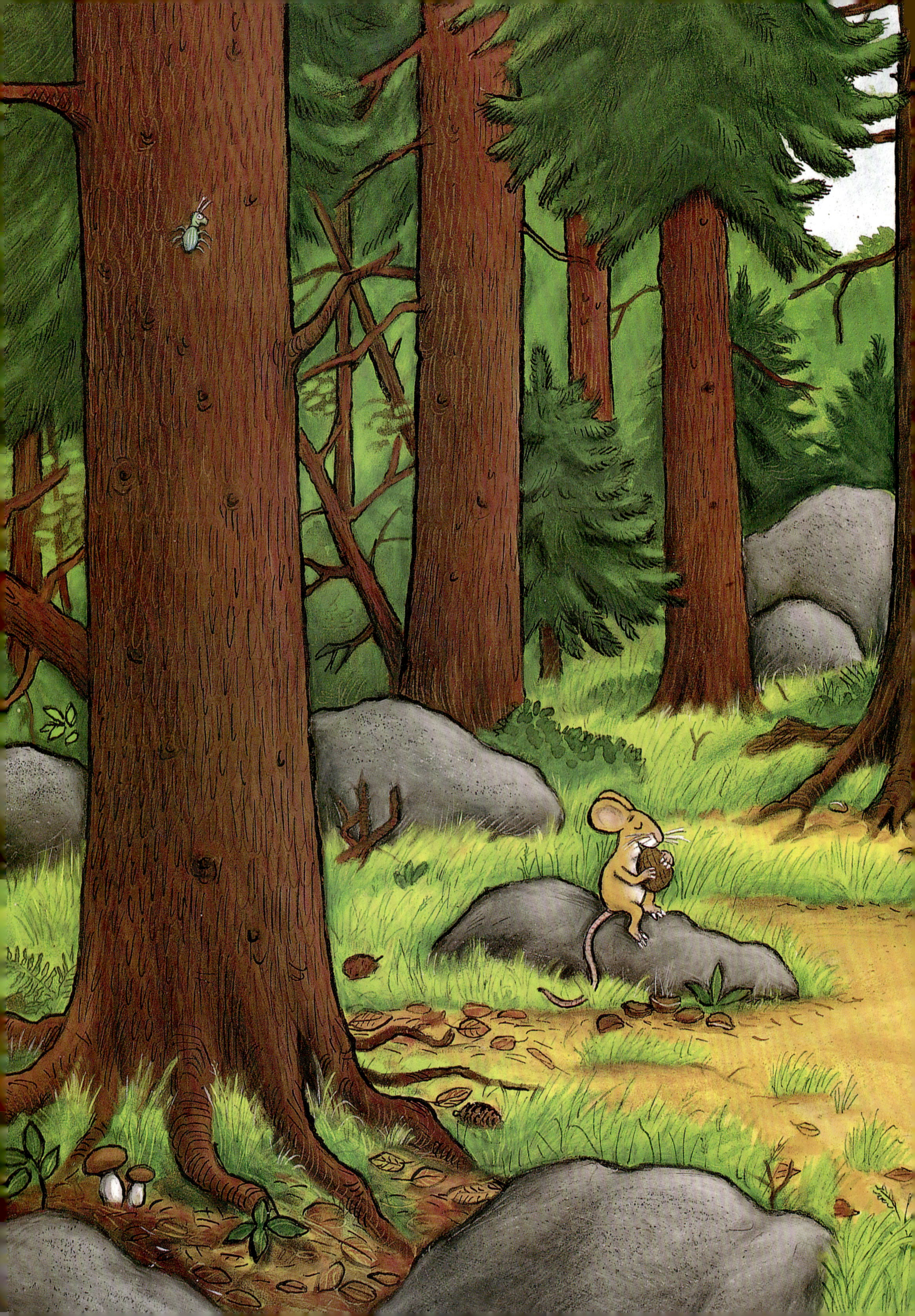

密林深处静悄悄。
小老鼠捧着榛果美美地嚼。
这榛果的味道真是好!

The Gruffalo

A mouse took a stroll through the deep dark wood.
A fox saw the mouse and the mouse looked good.
"Where are you going to, little brown mouse?
Come and have lunch in my underground house."
"It's terribly kind of you, Fox, but no –
I'm going to have lunch with a gruffalo."
"A gruffalo? What's a gruffalo?"
"A gruffalo! Why, didn't you know?

"He has terrible tusks, and terrible claws,
And terrible teeth in his terrible jaws."
"Where are you meeting him?"
"Here, by these rocks,
And his favourite food is roasted fox."

"Roasted fox! I'm off!" Fox said.
"Goodbye, little mouse," and away he sped.
"Silly old Fox! Doesn't he know,
There's no such thing as a gruffalo?"

On went the mouse through the deep dark wood.
An owl saw the mouse and the mouse looked good.
"Where are you going to, little brown mouse?
Come and have tea in my treetop house."
"It's frightfully nice of you, Owl, but no –
I'm going to have tea with a gruffalo."
"A gruffalo? What's a gruffalo?"
"A gruffalo! Why, didn't you know?

8   "He has knobbly knees, and turned-out toes,
And a poisonous wart at the end of his nose."
"Where are you meeting him?"
"Here, by this stream,
And his favourite food is owl ice cream."

9   "Owl ice cream? Toowhit toowhoo!
Goodbye, little mouse," and away Owl flew.
"Silly old Owl! Doesn't he know,
There's no such thing as a gruffalo?"

11   On went the mouse through the deep dark wood.
A snake saw the mouse and the mouse looked good.
"Where are you going to, little brown mouse?
Come for a feast in my logpile house."
"It's wonderfully good of you, Snake, but no –
I'm having a feast with a gruffalo."

"A gruffalo? What's a gruffalo?"
"A gruffalo! Why, didn't you know?

"His eyes are orange, his tongue is black;
He has purple prickles all over his back."
"Where are you meeting him?"
"Here, by this lake,
And his favourite food is scrambled snake."

"Scrambled snake! It's time I hid!
Goodbye, little mouse," and away Snake slid.
"Silly old Snake! Doesn't he know,
There's no such thing as a gruffal . . ."

". . . Oh!"
But who is this creature with terrible claws
And terrible teeth in his terrible jaws?

He has knobbly knees and turned-out toes
And a poisonous wart at the end of his nose.
His eyes are orange, his tongue is black;
He has purple prickles all over his back.

"Oh help! Oh no! It's a gruffalo!"

"My favourite food!" the Gruffalo said.
"You'll taste good on a slice of bread!"
"Good?" said the mouse. "Don't call me good!
I'm the scariest creature in this wood.
Just walk behind me and soon you'll see,
Everyone is afraid of me."

"All right," said the Gruffalo, bursting with laughter.
"You go ahead and I'll follow after."
They walked and walked till the Gruffalo said,
"I hear a hiss in the leaves ahead."

"It's Snake," said the mouse. "Why, Snake, hello!"
Snake took one look at the Gruffalo.
"Oh crumbs!" he said, "Goodbye, little mouse,"
And off he slid to his logpile house.

19 "You see?" said the mouse. "I told you so."
"Amazing!" said the Gruffalo.
They walked some more till the Gruffalo said,
"I hear a hoot in the trees ahead."

20 "It's Owl," said the mouse. "Why, Owl, hello!"
Owl took one look at the Gruffalo.
"Oh dear!" he said, "Goodbye, little mouse,"
And off he flew to his treetop house.

21 "You see?" said the mouse. "I told you so."
"Astounding!" said the Gruffalo.
They walked some more till the Gruffalo said,
"I can hear feet on the path ahead."

22 "It's Fox," said the mouse. "Why, Fox, hello!"
Fox took one look at the Gruffalo.
"Oh help!" he said, "Goodbye, little mouse,"
And off he ran to his underground house.

"Well, Gruffalo," said the mouse, "You see?
Everyone is afraid of me!
But now my tummy's beginning to rumble.
My favourite food is – gruffalo crumble!"
"*Gruffalo crumble!*" the Gruffalo said,
And quick as the wind he turned and fled.

All was quiet in the deep dark wood.
The mouse found a nut and the nut was good.

阅读经典图画书
感悟人生大智慧

我小 mouse 不是下饭下酒下茶的菜

——梅子涵（著名儿童文学作家，教授，儿童文学博士生导师）

小老鼠这智慧是被逼出来的。因为他只是一个小东西，所以人人都想把他当成下饭的菜、下酒的菜、甚至喝茶的菜。这真是一些很糟糕的家伙。而且他们还不明明白白地说，装文雅，让你被下饭了、下酒了、下茶了，还稀里糊涂。用请你吃饭、请你喝酒、请你喝茶的办法来吃你，真是阴险又平庸。别人会上当，我小 mouse 清醒着呢！

小老鼠的方法不叫欺骗。

对这一些不怀好意的人，你最好既别恳求，也别"诚实"。如果你恳求说，狐狸伯伯、猫头鹰叔叔、蛇哥，我知道你想吃我，求求你别吃吧，那么你还是被吃！如果你说，狐狸伯伯、猫头鹰叔叔、蛇哥，既然你要吃我，想用我下饭、下酒、下茶，那么你就请下吧，那么你立刻就片甲不留了。

长得这等模样的咕噜牛完全是小老鼠瞎编出来的。小老鼠没有想到，自己瞎编的咕噜牛竟然跑到自己跟前来了，要把自己吃掉！庆幸的是小老鼠瞎编的时候，只把咕噜牛的样子编得吓人，没顾上把他的头脑也编得出众。要不然，他跟在小老鼠的后面，所有的动物都是看见了他才吓得逃跑的，他怎么就看不见呢？

老鼠把所有想伤害他的家伙都吓跑了。他可不想伤害任何人。他也没有要得到许多东西的愿望。他只要有一个榛果吃吃，别饿着肚子就可以了。他的要求不高啊。所以树林里静悄悄，小老鼠的心里也一定静悄悄。静悄悄的小老鼠，还会遇见什么事呢？你看看，在吃着榛果的小老鼠很像是在想："我还会遇到什么事呢？管它的，还是吃榛果，吃榛果聪明。"

阅读经典图画书 透视艺术的幽默趣味

《咕噜牛》的图像演奏

——李茵茵（台湾台东大学儿童文学研究所博士）

拿到这部绘本，我们可以看到，它的封面就是一个故事——大怪物咕噜牛对上瘦小而灵巧的老鼠，你能看出他们彼此的关系吗？仔细看，主要角色——小老鼠出现在左下方，而与他有冲突的角色——咕噜牛则出现在它的右边，这是配合由左往右的阅读习惯。再注意他们的眼神：咕噜牛虽然身躯庞大、长相可怕，但是它的眼神里却透露出一丝憨傻劲儿；小老鼠悠然自得、小眼珠滴溜溜地转，仿佛在打什么鬼主意，暗示着这是一个小老鼠对咕噜牛，以智取胜的故事。

绘本的前环衬像是故事的背景，绿色的森林中洋溢着一种宁静的氛围。不过，要是你顺着地上的脚印和拔起的树根观察，就会发现岩石后面的森林充满不安和危险。再加上这两页与故事的最后两页相呼映衬，这两页就如同跟着脚印走进咕噜牛的想象；后两页在静谧的森林中只剩下小老鼠独自美美地享受着榛果，消除了对大怪物咕噜牛的恐惧，回到宁静与安详的绿色森林。

翻开扉页，圆形的背景映衬出主角的故事。机灵的小老鼠像在邀请图画外的我们，一起进入这个故事。

注意到了吗？阿克塞尔图画中的角色大都是圆形或柔软的线条，这改变了读者在接触负面角色时的不安和恐惧；在分述咕噜牛时，每一个部位都是局部的、夸张的，但组合在一起却难得的憨厚圆润，这加深了角色的趣味性与吸引力。随着故事的发展，每一段故事都有三段式的重复性图像，逐渐拔高了咕噜牛的形象。（1.用三角和尖锐的攻击性表现想吃小老鼠的动物，并映衬着小老鼠的孤单和瘦小；2.局部放大咕噜牛的各部位，以投射夸张其恐怖；3.用缩小的线框罩住逃跑的动物，压抑动物害怕咕噜牛的情绪。）直到书的中页用跨页拉大咕噜牛的气势，节奏再逐渐转缓，慢慢走出对咕噜牛的恐惧。这本书最妙的就是中页关键性的设计，带动了整本书的氛围与节奏。

在图画的演奏中，阿克塞尔掌握了文学性、音乐性、艺术性及浓浓的趣味性。这是一本值得品味再三的图画书。